MARK ZUCKERBERG

Success Secrets

VISIONARIES WHO CHANGED THE WORLD SERIES

MARK ZUCKERBERG

Success Secrets

VISIONARIES WHO CHANGED THE WORLD SERIES

George Ilian

JAICO PUBLISHING HOUSE

Ahmedabad Bangalore Bhopal Bhubaneswar Chennai
Delhi Hyderabad Kolkata Lucknow Mumbai

Published by Jaico Publishing House
A-2 Jash Chambers, 7-A Sir Phirozshah Mehta Road
Fort, Mumbai - 400 001
jaicopub@jaicobooks.com
www.jaicobooks.com

MARK ZUCKERBERG: SUCCESS SECRETS
ISBN 978-93-87944-80-0

First Jaico Impression: 2019

Content excerpted from
Top Visionaries Who Changed the World by George Ilian.

Page design and layout:
Special Effects Graphics Design Company, Mumbai

Printed by
Thomson Press (India) Limited

Contents

Introduction

At the age of just 31, Mark Zuckerberg was worth an estimated $46 billion. He had not inherited his wealth, but made it from scratch in only 12 years, and with the creation of a single product: Facebook.

Unless you have buried your head in the sand for the past decade, ignoring not only the internet but also newspapers, television, cinema, and water cooler discussions, you cannot have missed the social media phenomenon which is Facebook. It has an estimated 1.5 billion users, in almost every corner of the globe, and is the driving force behind Free Basics, an app which provides free internet services in the developing world.

Zuckerberg himself has not only made exorbitant wealth, leaving relatively little controversy in his wake, but also positioned himself at the forefront of enterprise and innovation. He has been voted as *Time* magazine's man of the year, and is the poster child for the tech world. Along with Bill Gates and Warren Buffet, men many years his senior, he was one of the key signatories to The Giving Pledge, and as a result he is leading the way for philanthropists. His subsequent promise to donate 99% of his Facebook shares to charity, during his lifetime, shows his level of commitment to this ideal.

The early chapters of this book are laid out roughly in chronological order: first of all, we discuss Zuckerberg's childhood and education; then his early forays into social media and programming; the birth and growth of Facebook; and his launch of Internet.org. In the second part of the book, we look more widely at his estimated wealth; awards and accolades; philanthropic efforts; political involvement; and, last but not least; his personal life.

Throughout the book you will find lessons we have drawn from Zuckerberg's life and work, which you can apply in your own life. Though not all of these lessons will be personally applicable, you can take inspiration from them, and put into practice those that are most relevant to you. You will find a summary of the overarching themes of those lessons – four unforgettable lessons from Mark Zuckerberg – in the book's conclusion.

One

Childhood and Education

Right from the word go, Mark Zuckerberg was a child prodigy, a fascinating and precocious child with seemingly infinite capacity to learn and innovate. Born on 14 May, 1984 in White Plains, New York, the son of two professional parents, dentist Edward Zuckerberg and psychiatrist Karen Kempner, Zuckerberg and his three sisters were raised in New York state, and then in New Hampshire.

↳ **A commitment to education, from an early age, stands you in good stead later in life.**

All the members of the Zuckerberg family were academically gifted, and professionally high achievers. Zuckerberg was no exception. At Phillips Exeter

Academy, a co-educational independent school for boarding and day students, Zuckerberg followed in the footsteps of numerous notable alumni, including Dan Brown, author of The Da Vinci Code; Lloyd Shapley, winner of the 2012 Nobel Prize in economics; and Adam D'Angelo, computer scientist and co-founder of the billion-dollar question and answer website, Quora. He won academic prizes in maths, astronomy, physics,. and classical studies, was captain of the fencing team, and by the time he applied to Harvard University, he could read and write French, Hebrew, Latin, and ancient Greek, in addition to his native English.

↳ **Don't ever be embarrassed about being smart, or about having a diverse range of interests.**

Zuckerberg's interest in computer programming began whilst he was still at middle school. He learned Atari BASIC programming from his father, then took private classes with software developer David Newman. Still in high school, Zuckerberg enrolled in a graduate class at the liberal arts college, Mercy College, in New York, and he built a number of programmes, including computer games illustrated by his friends; ZuckNet, a primitive version of AOL's Instant Messenger (released the following year), which enabled all the computers in his house to communicate with those in his father's dental practice; and the Synapse Media Player, which used machine learning to analyse and predict users' listening preferences. Zuckerberg's Synapse Media Player was featured in both *Slashdot* and *PC Magazine*, where it received a rating of 3/5 from reviewers.

> *"I got my first computer in the 6th grade or so. As soon as I got it, I was interested in finding out how it worked and how the programs worked and then figuring out how to write programs at just deeper and deeper levels within the system."*
>
> – Mark Zuckerberg

↳ It is never too soon to discover your passion and start developing your ideas.

Zuckerberg enrolled at Harvard University, signing up for classes in computer science and psychology. He belonged to the Alpha Epsilon Pi (AEΠ or AEPi) fraternity, which is based upon Jewish principles (Zuckerberg was raised Jewish; see: *Personal Life*), and notable members have included Nobel Prize winners, Olympic sportsmen, attorney generals, film makers, entrepreneurs, and even the inventor of Tinder. It was a network which would stand Zuckerberg in good stead as he pursued his own commercial ambitions. Zuckerberg also belonged to Kirkland House, an undergraduate house popular with Harvard's athletes.

↳ **The network of people around you has a significant impact on the likelihood that your projects will succeed.**

Although Zuckerberg is undoubtedly academically able, and passionate about his subjects, he did not complete his degree at Harvard. He decided instead to take a semester off from studying to concentrate on developing Facebook (see *Facebook*, below), then dropped out of the university entirely to devote his full attention to the company's growth.

> *"All of my friends who have younger siblings who are going to college or high school – my number one piece of advice is: You should learn how to program."*
>
> – Mark Zuckerberg

Two

Facebook

↪ A formal education at a university will not suit everyone.

As we saw in the section on *Childhood and Education*, Zuckerberg was accomplished at computer programming from an early age, and saw it as much as a means of entertainment as something which had commercial value. The programming skills he learned in his teenage years, honed at Harvard, and encouraged and inspired by the fellow students he met there, set him on the path to developing what is the financially most successful, and widely used, social media platform in the world: Facebook.

Early Experiments

As a sophomore student, Zuckerberg created CourseMatch, a simple program which enabled users to select courses (informed by the previous choices of other users), and to form study groups. It was his first attempt at social networking and, though not terribly exciting, it laid the groundwork for Zuckerberg's next project, Facemash.

↳ **Spend time experimenting with your ideas so that you hone your skills.**

A computerised variant of the *Hot or Not?* game, Zuckerberg built Facemash with three friends, Andrew McCollum, Chris Hughes, and Dustin Moskovitz. He took images from the online face books (student profiles) of nine Harvard Houses (halls of residence), and laid them side by side, two photos at a time. Users could then vote as to who was hot, and who was not. Zuckerberg launched the site on 28 October 2003, and wrote in his personal blog:

> *"I'm a little intoxicated, not gonna lie. So what if it's not even 10 pm and it's a Tuesday night? What? The Kirkland dormitory face book is open*

on my desktop and some of these people have pretty horrendous face book pics. I almost want to put some of these faces next to pictures of some farm animals and have people vote on which is more attractive."

– 2:49 pm

"Yea, it's on. I'm not exactly sure how the farm animals are going to fit into this whole thing (you can't really ever be sure with farm animals...), but I like the idea of comparing two people together."

– 11:10 am

"Let the hacking begin."

– 2:57 pm

↳ **You need to be excited about what you create. If an idea doesn't thrill you, it won't thrill anyone else either.**

The hacking was a reference to the fact that Zuckerberg had no ownership of the face books' content: the images the books contained were intended for reference purposes only, to help students identify one another. He had to hack the Harvard server in order to extract the images for his own site.

> *"The Hacker Way is an approach to building that involves continuous improvement and iteration. Hackers believe that something can always be better, and that nothing is ever complete."*
>
> – Mark Zuckerberg

Facemash was an immediate hit. Zuckerberg forwarded the site to several Harvard University servers one weekend, and by Monday it had to be shut down because its popularity had overwhelmed one of the network switches. When it was discovered what he had done, Zuckerberg faced charges of violating copyright, breach of security, and violating individual privacy, and faced expulsion from the university for his actions, but these charges against him were later dropped.

↳ Be aware of security and privacy laws.

Not one to let the site go entirely, however, he reformatted it for his art history final, uploading 500

Augustan images, and allowed classmates to share their notes in the comments section alongside each image. According to Zuckerberg's art history professor, the project had the best grades of any final he had ever given. This was Zuckerberg's first social hack.

The facemash.com URL was auctioned off to an unknown buyer for $30, 201 in October 2010.

Three

The Birth of Facebook

↳ **Be prepared to rework your ideas.**

> *"I literally coded Facebook in my dorm room and launched it from my dorm room. I rented a server for $85 a month, and I funded it by putting an ad on the side, and we've funded ever since by putting ads on the side."*
>
> – Mark Zuckerberg

His experience with Facemash taught Zuckerberg several important things. Interviewed in *The Harvard Crimson,* a widely read magazine on the university campus, he said:

It is clear that the technology needed to create a centralized website is readily available ... the benefits are many...Everyone's been talking a lot about a universal face book within Harvard. I think it's kind of silly that it would take the University a couple of years to get around to it as I can do it better than they can, and I can do it in a week.

He was aware of a need in the marketplace, that he had the skills to fulfil it, and that as he could fulfil that need faster than anyone else, he would have the first mover advantage. Zuckerberg wanted to create a website which would allow members of the university not only to see each other's images and profiles, but also to connect with one another. The idea for Facebook was born.

↳ The very best ideas are simple.

Zuckerberg started coding Facebook in January 2004. Unsure exactly how to promote his new site, he asked his friends for advice. His roommate, Dustin Moskovitz, remembers Facebook's entrance into the world like this:

When Mark finished the site, he told a couple of friends ... then one of them suggested putting it on the Kirkland House online mailing list, which was ...

300 people.... By the end of the night, we were ... actively watching the registration process. Within 24 hours, we had somewhere between 1200 and 1500 registrants.

↳ Poll your friends and other contacts about your ideas.

The Facebook, as it was then known, was an instant hit, but it was not without its problems. Three of Zuckerberg's fellow students at Harvard, Cameron Winklevoss, his brother Tyler Winklevoss, and Divya Narendra, all accused Zuckerberg of agreeing to help them build a social network called Harvard Connection, and then running off with their idea. They took their complaint to *The Harvard Crimson,* to get a voice amongst the university community at large, who began to investigate the matter.

↳ Be very careful who you talk to, and who you work with, during the early stage of your projects.

Zuckerberg was not about to sit by blindly whilst the investigation was taking place: he wanted to know what was going on so that he would be in a stronger position to respond. Using The Facebook, he was able to identify users who also worked at *The Harvard Crimson*. He cross-referenced their names with the list of failed logins to The Facebook, and then used those same passwords to try and access the users' Harvard email accounts. He successfully accessed two accounts, and was thus able to read their communications as the investigation progressed. Three of the users subsequently brought a lawsuit against Zuckerberg for this abuse of trust and breach of privacy, but the case was settled.

When The Facebook was launched, it was only available to members of Harvard University. You had to have a Harvard email address to sign up. This, whether deliberate or not, was a shrewd move, as a social network can only work if it has sufficient penetration within a group of people. People will only join if their friends have already joined, or if they expect to find people they know, and this is far easier to achieve if the pool of people is small. In the first month after The Facebook was launched, half of Harvard's undergraduate population had signed up. The appetite for the site was proven, and its model was working.

Four

The Facebook's Founders

↳ **Launch your products in a market you understand.**

To date, The Facebook had been more or less a one-man band. It was Zuckerberg's baby. But he wasn't arrogant: he knew that in order for the project to grow and realise its full potential, he had to bring other people onboard. He recruited four colleagues from amongst his social circle at Harvard to help him develop and promote The Facebook further.

Each of Zuckerberg's new recruits had their own area of expertise and responsibility. Eduardo Saverin, a Brazilian student who was president of the Harvard Investment Association, had already proven his business skills by making a $300,000 profit from strategic investments in the Brazilian oil industry. He became The Facebook's chief financial officer and business manager. It was Saverin's money, along with Zuckerberg's, which sustained the company during its first few months, and both men took equity stakes in the company.

Zuckerberg's roommate, Dustin Moskovitz, who had been there, watching, the night Zuckerberg launched The Facebook, came onboard as a programmer. He was the company's first chief technology officer and then vice president of engineering, and in March 2011 *Forbes* magazine would declare him to be the youngest self-made billionaire in history. He was just 26 years old.

Andrew McCollum did the graphic design work. He worked at the company for its first three years, then returned to Harvard University to complete his undergraduate degree, and then to do a Masters.

The final member of this founding team was Chris Hughes. He had met Zuckerberg during his freshman year in 2002, and beta tested many of Zuckerberg's early designs, as well as making product suggestions. Hughes became The Facebook's spokesman, and it was his idea to open the site to schools, paving its way for global expansion. He travelled with The Facebook team to Palo Alto in the summer of 2004, but unlike his colleagues, decided to return to Harvard to complete his degree. He would rejoin them in California after his graduation in 2006.

Five

The Growth of Facebook

↳ **Even if you are the person with the original idea, you don't have to develop it alone, and should avoid even trying to do so.**

My goal was never to just create a company. A lot of people misinterpret that, as if I don't care about revenue or profit or any of those things. But what not being just a company means to me is not being just that – building something that actually makes a really big change in the world.

– Mark Zuckerberg

The Facebook's expansion began in March 2004, when the site was opened up to students at the universities of Columbia, Stanford, and Yale. The utility of the network, combined with the sense of exclusivity – you had to be at one of these elite universities to join – made it instantly popular.

↪ Exclusivity is a powerful marketing tool as you can create demand for a product before it is even available.

In the summer of 2004, Zuckerberg and his colleagues travelled to Palo Alto, in the centre of Silicon Valley. They incorporated The Facebook as a company, and Sean Parker, co-founder of the file sharing site Napster, became the company's first president. He had already been advising Zuckerberg informally for some time, and he convinced Zuckerberg and his colleagues (barring Hughes, see above) to stay. Venture capitalist Peter Thiel, who had made his money as the co-founder of PayPal alongside Elon Musk, made a $500,000 angel investment in exchange for a 10.2% equity stake in The Facebook. Other seed round investments were made by Reid Hoffman, CEO of LinkedIn; entrepreneur Mark Pincus, who had sold his first start-up, Freeloader, Inc., for $38 million and would later found online games company Zynga; and Maurice Werdegar of Western Technology Investment.

“*By giving people the power to share, we’re making the world more transparent.*”

—Mark Zuckerberg

↳ Even digital businesses need to have a physical home.

The Facebook was supposed to take off in 2005. It now had its base in Palo Alto, where tech entrepreneurs and investors were two a penny, yet all excited about Zuckerberg's idea. He dropped the "The" from The Facebook's name, and henceforth the company was simply Facebook. The company opened out to 21 universities in the United Kingdom (Oxford and Cambridge first amongst them, in keeping with the idea that this was a network for elite university students and alumni); they launched a version for high schools, which was by invitation only; and additional networks were created for the employees of Apple, Microsoft, and other major tech companies. By the end of the year Facebook was available to more than 2,000 colleges and universities, and 25,000 high schools, in the United States, Canada, the United Kingdom, Ireland, Australia, New Zealand, and Mexico. The company raised $12.7 million in venture capital from Accel Partners, valuing Facebook at $98 million.

↳ A company cannot grow without money, either from income that it has generated, or from investors.

In summer 2006, Facebook opened up to anyone

around the world, so long as they were aged 13 and older, and had a valid email address. Zuckerberg closed Facebook's Series B funding round with investments from Greylock Partners and Meritech Capital, as well as additional funds from Thiel and Accel Partners. The valuation of Facebook stood at $500 million, not bad for 18 months' work.

> *"I mean, we've built a lot of products that we think are good, and will help people share photos and share videos and write messages to each other. But it's really all about how people are spreading Facebook around the world in all these different countries. And that's what's so amazing about the scale that it's at today."*
>
> – Mark Zuckerberg

Sales Negotiations and Profitability

Facebook had grown very quickly, and it seemed inevitable that Zuckerberg and his co-founders would want to realise their investment, selling out at least part of their stakes as soon as possible. Facebook's main competitor, MySpace, was sold to News Corp in 2005, and market analysts thought Zuckerberg would avail himself of a similar exit strategy. In quick succession, however, Zuckerberg turned down a $750 million offer from an unknown bidder, and a $1 billion offer from Yahoo!, Microsoft suggested it would make a $300–500 million investment in exchange for a 5% stake, and Google followed suit. But Zuckerberg wasn't interested. He wanted to keep Facebook independent, stating:

We're not really looking to sell the company... We're not looking to *IPO* anytime soon. It's just not the core focus of the company.

His view may well have been shaped by the fact that Thiel had already created an internal valuation of $8 billion for Facebook, based on its predicted revenues. Microsoft was allowed to invest $240 million for a 1.6% stake, implying a valuation of $15 billion, and Hong Kong billionaire Li Ka-shing invested a further $60 million.

➥ Every company must have an exit strategy.

The interesting thing is that all of these investments were speculative: Facebook had a huge network of users, but they paid no subscription fees, and the site generated almost no revenue. Zuckerberg was quite open about his failure to monetise the site, saying:

I don't think social networks can be monetized in

the same way that search did ... In three years from now we have to figure out what the optimum model is. But that is not our primary focus today.

For Facebook's board members, monetisation was a priority, however. The board recruited Sheryl Sandberg, Vice President of Global Online Sales and Operations at Google, as Facebook's chief operating officer in 2008. Zuckerberg had known Sandberg for just a few months, having met her at a Christmas drinks party and then again at the World Economic Forum in Davos, but he was convinced she was the perfect fit for the role. He wasn't wrong.

↪ A company has to make a profit: that is its purpose.

Sandberg was the first woman in a senior role at Facebook. As far as she was concerned, the company was "primarily interested in building a really cool site; profits, they assumed, would follow." Sandberg decided a more proactive approach was required. She brainstormed ideas with Facebook employees, and concluded that advertising revenues would be the main source of monetisation. The board agreed with her findings, and Sandberg changed the company's advertising model. As a result, Facebook had positive cash flow for the very first time in September 2009.

"Advertising works most effectively when it's in line with what people are already trying to do. And people are trying to communicate in a certain way on Facebook – they share information with their friends, they learn about what their friends are doing – so there's really a whole new opportunity for a new type of advertising model within that."

– Mark Zuckerberg

Six

Acquisitions

“In terms of doing work and in terms of learning and evolving as a person, you just grow more when you get more people’s perspectives, I really try and live the mission of the company and keep everything else in my life extremely simple.”

—Mark Zuckerberg

↳ **If you are unsure about how to develop your income streams, or even what those streams should be, ask for expert advice.**

Once Facebook became profitable, it was in a position to start investing in other companies, and to make wholesale acquisitions when it was useful to do so. These acquisitions were usually of competing products, or services which could be added to Facebook's portfolio to make their own offering more attractive.

↳ You do not need to build every aspect of your company from scratch.

Examples of early acquisitions include FriendFeed, a real-time news feed aggregator which brought together users' feeds from multiple social media platforms, blogs, etc. and was the brainchild of Bret Taylor (co-creator of Google Maps) and Paul Buchheit (the lead developer of Gmail, who also prototyped Google AdSense); Octazen Solutions, a Malaysian start-up whose software could be used to import contacts from multiple sources; photo sharing system Divvyshot; and the team behind Storylane, a start-up which allowed users to share their interests with a given community.

Such acquisitions made Facebook increasingly attractive to investors as they enriched the platform's portfolio and technical capacity. After the company had its IPO in February 2012 (see *IPO*, below) Facebook had a much larger pool of cash to draw from, and the board decided to make two further, phenomenal acquisitions: Instagram and WhatsApp Inc.

↳ Only buy into other companies which enhance your core offering.

First released in October 2010, Instagram is a social

network focused on photo and video sharing. It's square, Polaroid-style images were distinctive (though in later versions of the app alternative aspect ratios were also popular), and users also liked the fact that they could add filters to their images. The free app had 100 million users in its first 18 months, and in April 2012, Facebook acquired Instagram for $1 billion in cash and stock. It was a shrewd investment: Instagram trebled its number of users over the next two-year period, a rate of growth which even Facebook itself could not match.

↪ **If you see a company which has significant growth potential, and is cash generative, think about adding it to your portfolio.**

Although Facebook paid a gargantuan sum for Instagram, it would shell out even more money for messaging service WhatsApp. Created by two former employees of Yahoo!, who had ironically enough been turned down for jobs at Facebook, WhatsApp launched in November 2009. By spring 2014, it had 500 million users a month, and today that figure is estimated at around 1 billion users. Facebook acquired WhatsApp in February 2014 for $19 billion, of which $4 billion was paid in cash, $12 billion was in Facebook shares, and the remaining $3 billion was in restricted stock options for WhatsApp's founders.

↳ Communications are key to everyday life.

Immediately after the acquisition of WhatsApp, Zuckerberg gave the keynote address at the Mobile World Congress in Barcelona. He explained that the acquisition of WhatsApp was a key component of his Internet.org vision (see *Internet.org*), later explaining in an interview with TechCrunch that:

The idea… is to develop a group of basic internet services that would be free of charge to use 'a 911 for the internet.' These could be a social networking service like Facebook, a messaging service, maybe search and other things like weather. Providing a bundle of these free of charge to users will work like a gateway drug of sorts – users who may be able to afford data services and phones these days just don't see the point of why they would pay for those data services. This would give them some context for why they are important, and that will lead them to paying for more services like this – or so the hope goes.

↪ Even if you think that something you have done, or plan to do, is a good idea, you need to be able to explain it in a cohesive, convincing way to other people.

Developments in WhatsApp subsequent to the application's acquisition by Facebook include the ability to handle voice calls, and the dropping of its annual $1 subscription charge. Both of these changes increased its appeal to customers, with *Forbes* magazine predicting that WhatsApp and Skype would have lost conventional communications companies a combined total of $386 billion between 2012 and 2018. Facebook and its subsidiaries, once again, are changing the way in which we communicate, and in which money is made.

Initial Public Offering (IPO)

Despite Zuckerberg's own initial resistance to the idea of an IPO (see *Sales Negotiations and Profitability*), it was inevitable that Facebook would one day have a public share offering: a single company could not afford to buy Facebook in its entirety, and yet the investors had to somehow to realise their investment.

Zuckerberg's leadership, and conviction about

the potential of Facebook, was essential because it enabled him to grow the company to well beyond the size estimated, and valuation offered, by Yahoo!, Microsoft, and Google. His confidence, and his faith in his product, paid off, and by ensuring that he assembled around himself a world-class team, he was able to gain the largest valuation to date for a newly public company. Facebook's IPO raised $16 billion, making it the third largest in US history.

So how did it happen? What steps did Zuckerberg take?

By resisting both buyouts and taking the company public for a protracted period, Zuckerberg was able to grow Facebook (increasing its ultimate valuation), and create an appetite in the marketplace for its shares: numerous investors wanted a piece of the action, but couldn't buy in, and this made the company even more tantalising. He told *PC Magazine* in 2010, "we are definitely in no rush."

↳ Bide your time.

On 1 February, 2012, Zuckerberg filed Facebook's S1 document with the US Securities and Exchange Commission in Washington DC. Key points of the document were an outline of the company's current position (845 million active monthly users; 2.7 billion daily likes and comments; and an increasing but decelerating increase in the number of users and income); a statement that Zuckerberg would retain 22% of Facebook's shares, but 57% of the voting shares; and an indication that Facebook expected to raise $5 billion from the IPO. It would therefore be one of the largest IPOs in history.

Zuckerberg personally led the roadshow for the Facebook IPO, and he did it in his own inimitable way. He turned up at the first investors' meeting wearing a hoodie, not a suit, which caused consternation in more conservative business circles, and generated plenty of column inches. Perhaps that was the idea of it. One investor described the move (which may or may not have been deliberate) as a "mark of immaturity," but it could also be seen as Zuckerberg reminding would-be investors that the ball was in his court, and he would run the roadshow and the IPO as he saw fit: he didn't need the money, and therefore had power.

↳ **You need to strike a careful balance between being yourself, and doing what investors and customers expect.**

Valuations of Facebook fluctuated significantly

during this period, though overall they increased. The low initial estimate was $28 to $35 per share, but this was quickly revised up to $34 to $38 per share. This top estimate gave a total valuation for the company of $104 billion, and yet there was still strong demand from would-be investors, especially from retail investors. The previous strong performance of Google and LinkedIn have investor's confidence, and no one wanted to risk missing out.

↪ You can make predictions about how your company will fare based on the performance of other similar companies, though this is by no means a fail-safe strategy.

Two days before the IPO, Zuckerberg announced that due to high demand, 25% more shares would be released. The stock would debut with 421 million shares. Some analysts did express concern, thinking that the estimates overvalued Facebook, especially given concerns about the company's advertising model: just days before the IPO, General Motors announced publicly it was going to cancel its $10 million advertising campaign on Facebook due to underperformance.

The Facebook IPO was fascinating to watch as

it was a cultural event as much as a business one: *Reuters* declared it to be “a cultural phenomenon”, and Zuckerberg, ever the showman, ran a series of events in the run up to the IPO. The night before it was due to take place, he led an all-night hackathon; CBS coined the word Zuckonomics to describe the way in which the IPO was playing out; and Zuckerberg rang a bell in the Facebook campus’s Hackers Square to announce, in a time-honoured fashion, that the company was going public.

↳ Even fairly standard financial transactions can appear exciting if marketed in the right way.

Trading in Facebook shares was due to begin at 11 a.m. on 18 May 2012, but it was delayed by half an hour due to technical issues at NASDAQ. This didn’t bode well, as there were to be technical glitches throughout the day, and buyers couldn’t always see whether or not their trades had been successful. The opening share price had been set at $38, and shot up as high as $45, but Facebook couldn’t maintain this price. When the price fell below $38, the underwriters had to wade in to keep the price steady, and the day’s trading closed with a disappointing share price of just $38.23. The stock did set a new record for the trading volume of an IPO

(460 million shares), and it raised $16 billion. The IPO confirmed Zuckerberg's own stake as being worth $19 billion, so all in all, it wasn't a bad day for him.

↳ Be prepared to be pleasantly surprised on some occasions, and sorely disappointed on others.

In the fortnight following the IPO, Facebook's share price declined. Trading curbs were used to slow the decline, but Facebook closed its first full week of trading down at $31.91, and after two weeks, the share price was just $27.72. It would be four weeks before the company made a modest gain, and when the *Wall Street Journal* described the IPO as a fiasco, they weren't the only ones holding that opinion. More than 40 legal suits against Facebook's lead underwriters, Morgan Stanley, JP Morgan, and Goldman Sachs, followed, with Morgan Stanley being forced to settle allegations of improperly influencing research analysts for $5 million. The reputation of both Morgan Stanley (the primary underwriter) and NASDAQ was damaged due to the botching of the IPO.

Those investors who did keep their Facebook shares (and nerve), rather than dumping them in panic and fury shortly after the IPO, made a shrewd decision. Today the share price stands at $111, and it has been growing consistently since it hit an all-time low of $18.06 in August 2012. The current forecast, drawn from 54 polled investment analysts, is that Facebook will outperform the market in the coming year, and they have a median 12-month target of $135, with some predicting the share price could go as high as $170 by the end of that period. It seems that the IPO wasn't such a fiasco after all.

➥ You need to be in business for the long haul.

Legal Disputes

The extraordinary success of Facebook, and the wealth which the company has generated for Zuckerberg, have meant, perhaps inevitably, that there are plenty of people who are extremely jealous of what he has received. Some of them believe that they are entitled to a slice of the Facebook pie for the early involvement or ideas; others are just chancing their luck. Whatever the background, such individuals are canny enough to realise that whether their claim is valid or not, simply making allegations will quite likely catapult them into the limelight, giving them their 30 seconds of fame. For the Winklevoss brothers, that period of fame has lasted even longer, though it hasn't exactly shown them in a good light.

> *"When I was in college I did a lot of stupid things and I don't want to make an excuse for that. Some of the things that people accuse me of are true, some of them aren't. There are pranks, IMs."*
>
> – Mark Zuckerberg

From the week of Facebook's launch, until June 2008, Zuckerberg was at loggerheads with twins Cameron and Tyler Winklevoss, and their classmate Divya Narendra, all three of whom had studied alongside him at Harvard. The plaintiffs alleged that they had hired Zuckerberg in 2003 to help them build a campus dating site called Harvard Connection, but that he had stalled their project and ultimately stolen their idea, turning it in to Facebook. Zuckerberg filed countersuit, accusing the plaintiffs of unfair business practices, and the case was settled out of court.

↳ Be prepared for people you have worked with in the past to turn against you when you start to taste success.

But the story doesn't end there. The settlement was based on stock, and by extension, Facebook's valuation. The plaintiffs argued that Zuckerberg had fraudulently misrepresented the value of Facebook stock, and took him back to court. It was a public relations nightmare, and one which Zuckerberg surely thought he had seen the back of.

Thankfully for Zuckerberg, Judge James Ware of Federal District Court in San Jose sided with Zuckerberg, enforcing the earlier decision. The judge noted that the plaintiffs were upset that Facebook's valuation was not the $15 billion that recent media reports had suggested, but that Facebook's own valuation was fair. He also suggested that the Winklevoss twins' father, Howard Winklevoss, was the main force behind the dispute. The Winklevosses and Narendra took their handout and slunk away, and Facebook issued the following statement:

We are happy that Judge Ware enforced the agreement settling our dispute with the ConnectU founders [ConnectU is the company founded by the Winklevoss twins]. ConnectU's founders were represented by six lawyers and a professor at Wharton

Business School when they signed the settlement agreement. The ConnectU founders understood the deal they made, and we are gratified that the court rejected their false allegations of fraud. Their challenge was simply a case of "buyer's remorse," as described by the Boston court earlier this month.

We were disappointed that we had to litigate the settlement, as we believed we were caught in the middle of a fee dispute between ConnectU's founders and its former counsel. Nevertheless, we can now consider this chapter closed and wish the Winklevoss brothers the best of luck in their future endeavors.

↪ When you win, be gracious, and humble.

The sincerity of that final clause may be questionable, because as you might imagine, there is no love lost between Zuckerberg and the Winklevoss twins. Their original idea might in some way have contributed to Zuckerberg's formulation of Facebook, but even if the Harvard Connection had been successful, and Facebook never even born, it was so limited in its scope and application that it could never have realised even a fraction of the growth that Facebook has seen. Unadulterated greed and jealousy are the driving forces behind their law suits, nothing more.

The Winklevoss twins were not the only people to claim Zuckerberg had acted in a less than honorable fashion. The co-founder of Facebook, Eduardo Saverin, had a claim to make too, and in his case it was rather more valid.

As well as putting his own money into the project, Saverin was Facebook's first chief financial officer and business manager (see *Facebook and its Founders*). In 2012, *Business Insider* magazine obtained a private email sent by Zuckerberg suggesting that he had knowingly cut Saverin out of Facebook in 2005, and diluted his stake in the company. Saverin's exit was central to the plot of the 2010 film, *The Social Network*, but even the film's writers could not have anticipated this particular turn of events.

The email, copied below, made Zuckerberg's intentions, and the impact on Saverin, clear.

> *[Redacted] "This email should probably be attorney-client privileged, not quite [sure] how to do that though.*
>
> *Anyhow, Sean and I have agreed that a price of one-half cent per share is the way to go for now. We think we can maybe almost justify and if not, we'll just deal with it later.*
>
> *We also agreed that if the company bonusing us*

the amount we need for the shares, plus tax, is a good solution to the problem of us all being completely broke. As far as Eduardo goes, I think it's safe to ask for his permission to make grants. Especially if we do it in conjunction with raising money. It's probably even OK to say how many shares we're adding to the pool. It's probably less OK to tell him who's getting the shares, just because he might have adverse reaction initially. But I think we may even be able to make him understand that. Is there a way to do this without making it painfully apparent to him that he's being diluted to 10%?

OK, that's all for now. I'll send you the list of grants I need made in another email in a second. Sean can send you grants for his people when he stops coughing up his lungs.

Hope you guys both feel better,

– Mark Zuckerberg"

His lawyer's response made it explicitly clear to Zuckerberg that as Saverin would be the only shareholder diluted by the grants issuances, he would have a legitimate claim to Facebook breaching fiduciary duty, and recommended that to avoid this happening, Zuckerberg should get Saverin's consent for the issuances in writing. Zuckerberg did not heed his advice, and Saverin successfully sued Facebook for approximately 5% of the company. At the IPO, that stake was work around $5 billion.

↳ Treat those you work with fairly.

A number of smaller lawsuits have also been brought against Facebook, by users and their representatives. A brief summary of two of the more interesting cases have been provided below.

Lane v Facebook was a class action challenging Facebook's privacy settings. When Facebook launched Beacon (which broadcast users' purchases from Facebook's affiliate sites), the default privacy settings required users to opt out, rather than to opt in. Many users were unaware of this fact, and as their purchases were then broadcast to their social and professional networks via their Facebook newsfeed, they felt that their privacy had been breached. The lawyers representing the plaintiffs claimed that Facebook had broken Electronic Communications Privacy Act, Video Privacy Protection Act, and California Consumer Legal Remedies Act, and also violated the violated the California Computer Crime Law and the Computer Fraud and Abuse Act. Facebook denied wrongdoing but did establish a cash settlement fund of $9.5 million. This was used to open and run a privacy foundation designed to educate users. Facebook terminated the Beacon program, paid the lawyers' fees, and made small compensation payments ($1,000 to $15,000) to the class representatives.

↳ **Legal cases can be expensive, and even if they don't upset your firm financially, they do no good for your reputation in the public eye.**

In recent years, Facebook has collaborated with academics to conduct a number of experiments on its users. These include "A 61-Million-Person Experiment in Social Influence and Political Mobilization," which Facebook ran during the 2010 Presidential election in the US; and "Emotional Contagion Through Social Networks", a controversial study in 2014 which manipulated the balance of positive and negative messages which 700,000 users saw. The study was criticised for its ethics, causing the privacy watchdog group Electronic Privacy Information Center (EPIC) to file a formal complaint with the Federal Trade. They alleged that Facebook had conducted the study without the knowledge or consent of their users, and secretly conducted a psychological experiment on their emotions, breaching their privacy. The outcome of this case is as yet undecided, but the law professor James Grimmelmann has stated that he believes the action is "illegal, immoral, and mood-altering".

Seven

Internet.org

↳ **The ethics of research is a mine field.**

> *"There is a huge need and a huge opportunity to get everyone in the world connected, to give everyone a voice and to help transform society for the future. The scale of the technology and infrastructure that must be built is unprecedented, and we believe this is the most important problem we can focus on."*
>
> – Mark Zuckerberg

With billions of dollars in personal wealth, not to mention command of the Facebook platform, Zuckerberg has to decide what his legacy will be. He's only in his early 30s, and will unlikely be inclined, or able, to replicate the commercial success of Facebook, but that doesn't mean he is unable to make world-altering changes in other fields. We will talk about his charitable giving in the section titled *Philanthropy*, but potentially far wider reaching is his Internet.org initiative.

Internet.org is a partnership between Facebook and Ericsson, MediaTek, Nokia, Opera Software, Qualcomm, and Samsung. It was launched in August 2013, and Zuckerberg issued a 10-page white paper, and gave a detailed video interview for TechCrunch, elaborating on the idea.

↳ **If you achieve a position of dominance in any given market, you can leverage that position to bring on board partners to help you achieve more than you would be capable of doing alone.**

Put simply, Zuckerberg believes that "connectivity is a human right," and that basic web servers should be available worldwide for free. The first Internet.org summit was held in October 2014 in India, where Zuckerberg met with the Indian Prime Minister Narendra Modi to discuss the project.

Internet.org provides free internet services

through an app called Free Basics. Although on the face of it, it is an admirable initiative with much to recommend it, it has its detractors, and their concerns do have some basis.

↳ No idea is without flaws.

Firstly, critics argue that Internet.org violates net neutrality. Facebook is, in essence, an unregulated gatekeeper to the Free Basics platform, deciding which services will and will not be provided on it. Facebook's rivals might well be discriminated against.

To date, more than a dozen countries are offering Free Basics, delivering it through approved mobile network providers. The service was launched in India in October 2015, but Zuckerberg was, perhaps unfairly, accused of targeting India's poor with Facebook proxies. The Telecom Regulatory Authority of India (TRAI) banned the service in the country just a year after its launch on the grounds that Free Basics' commercials were misleading, and they had masked the identity of its supporters in a manner nicknamed "astroturfing" (the deceptive practice of presenting an orchestrated marketing or public relations campaign in the guise of unsolicited comments from members of the public).

↪ **You need to tread carefully with regulatory bodies, carefully researching their remit, and building relationships with their decision makers.**

To date, the Internet.org project has brought an estimated 19 million new internet users online. Kids are able to do their homework and enhance their education, entrepreneurs are able to establish, expand and market their businesses, and more people are able to learn about keeping healthy, their rights, and the world around them. Any app can be offered on the platform so long as it meets Free Basics' guidelines, granting developers access to vast new markets in the developing world.

Eight

Wealth

↳ When you do good, you can also earn benefits for yourself.

In December 2015, *Business Insider* magazine estimated Zuckerberg's personal wealth (including his shareholding in Facebook) at $46 billion. He made nearly $12 billion of that wealth in 2015 alone. As his salary from Facebook is just $1 a year, this increase was driven almost entirely by Facebook's rising share price, though he has made personal investments in companies such as Mastery Connect ($5 million), Alt School ($100 million), Vicarious ($52 million), and Panorama Education ($4 million), as well. Since 2010, Time magazine has declared him as one of the 100 wealthiest and most influential people in the world, and his income stream looks as though it will only increase in the coming years.

Nine

Awards and Accolades

Unusually for a billionaire, Zuckerberg hasn't actively courted awards and accolades. He is satisfied with running his company the way he wants to, and to generate vast sums of money from doing so.

But awards have come his way: his achievements are so remarkable that they cannot be ignored. In 2010, he was named 'Person of the Year' by *Time* magazine, and *The Jerusalem Post* followed up with a similar accolade the following year, declaring him as one of the 'Most Influential Jews'. In 2016, Zuckerberg was nominated as CEO of the Year at the 9th Annual Crunchies Award, TechCrunch's recognition of the leaders in the tech field, and won the award in spite of stiff competition from Tim Cook (Apple), Jack Dorsey (Twitter/Square), Susan Wojcicki (YouTube), and Elon Musk (Tesla).

↳ **You will only be considered truly successful if you are recognised outside your specific sector, and gain general acclaim.**

For a self-proclaimed geek like Zuckerberg, one of his proudest moments is likely to be his cameo appearance on *The Simpsons.* In the "Loan-A-Lisa" episode, Lisa takes Nelson to a start-up event to meet successful founders, in the hope that they will inspire him to stay on in education rather than dropping out to run his business. Unfortunately for Lisa, the founders they meet are Zuckerberg, Bill Gates, and Richard Branson, none of whom completed their degrees. The episode aired in October 2010, two days after the release of *The Social Network,* and it was watched by an estimated 8.63 million households in the US. Critics agreed it was generally entertaining, though by no means the most hilarious, or insightful, of *The Simpsons*' episodes.

Ten

Philanthropy

↳ **Be prepared to laugh at yourself.**

> *"A squirrel dying in front of your house may be more relevant to your interests right now than people dying in Africa."*
>
> – Mark Zuckerberg

Coming from a very ordinary background, and having achieved great things as a result of his own education and the educational background of his parents, Zuckerberg was never going to be the spoilt rich kid. He has worked for his money, and understands acutely how much power it gives him. His early donations included an undisclosed sum to

Diaspora, an open-source personal web server; and $100 million to the public schools system in Newark. Modest, Zuckerberg wanted to make the latter donation anonymous, but New Jersey's Governor, Chris Christie, and Newark's Mayor, Cory Booker, convinced him to go public.

↳ Although you shouldn't boast about your generosity, there is no need to hide it either.

In 2010, Zuckerberg decided to sign 'The Giving Pledge', a commitment to give at least 50% of his wealth to charity, and to give it during his lifetime. Other signatories of the pledge include Bill Gates and Warren Buffet. The reason for spending before you die are numerous, and include the ability to decide which projects you support, to leverage your own professional network and skills to maximise the positive outcomes of the donations, and the reduction in administration costs if you don't have to use a succession of trust vehicles and lawyers to make decisions for you.

↪ If you make money, you have a responsibility to give back to the community which has helped you succeed, and do so in as effective a manner as possible.

Since signing the pledge, Zuckerberg has donated 18 million Facebook shares (with a value totalling $990 million) to the Silicon Valley Community Foundation, the largest community foundation in the US, which makes grants to domestic and international charities working in community building, economic security, education, immigration, and widening opportunities; and he also gave $25 million to help combat the spread of the Ebola virus in 2014.

Chan Zuckerberg Initiative

> *"The question I ask myself like almost every day is, 'Am I doing the most important thing I could be doing?"*
>
> – Mark Zuckerberg

Zuckerberg's daughter, Max, was born on 1 December 2015, and a week later Zuckerberg and his wife,

Priscilla Chan (see *Personal Life*) marked the occasion by publishing an open letter to their child. In the letter, they pledged to donate 99% of their Facebook shares (valued at the time at around $45 billion) to a new foundation, the Chan Zuckerberg Initiative. The foundation works in health and education, and the money will be spent over the course of Chan and Zuckerberg's lifetimes.

↳ Changes in your personal and professional life can significantly alter your outlook on life.

Technically the Chan Zuckerberg Initiative is neither a private foundation nor a charity: it is a limited liability company. This means that it is able to generate a profit, to lobby government bodies, and to make political donations. This model has drawn some criticism, as the donations Zuckerberg makes to the initiative will be tax deductible. In the words of Michael Miello at *The Daily Beast*, "If purity is the essence here, there seems no reason that the tax system should support it. Zuckerberg can afford to dabble in politics and society without massive subsidies from the rest of the country."

The published mission of the Chan Zuckerberg Initiative is to "advance human potential and promote equality in areas such as health, education, scientific research and energy". Zuckerberg and Chan intend to take the long view, targeting their resources at the biggest challenges they expect the next generation to face. The timeframe for their work is clear, as in the open letter they wrote:

Consider disease. Today we spend about 50 times more as a society treating people who are sick than we invest in research so you won't get sick in the first place...

Medicine has only been a real science for less than 100 years, and we've already seen complete cures for some diseases and good progress for others. As technology accelerates, we have a real shot at preventing, curing or managing all or most of the rest in the next 100 years.

↪ Put your money and your influence behind issues you really care about.

The Chan Zuckerberg Initiative is just a few years old, so we cannot yet see its impact on the causes which Chan and Zuckerberg clearly feel so strongly about. Hopefully, we will see the budding of something great, and in a decade or so, real, positive changes will be visible.

Eleven

Political Involvement

Politically, Zuckerberg is a pragmatist. He does not appear to have any particularly strong ideological leanings, and as he has never specified his own political views, there are those who would place him in both the conservative and liberal camps. It is likely, and indeed a shrewd business move, that he supports those politicians and parties best able to represent the commercial interests of Facebook, and the philanthropic interests of the Chan Zuckerberg Initiative, at the current moment in time.

↳ **There is no shame in being a pragmatist.**

That is not to say that Zuckerberg doesn't get involved in politics. In February 2013, he hosted his first fundraising event, for New Jersey Governor Chris Christie. Zuckerberg knew Christie from the time of his $100 million donation to Newark's public schools (see *Philanthropy*), and later that year he would run a similar fundraiser for Cory Booker. On both of these occasions, Zuckerberg's own interest was pushing for education reform, and he believed that these two men would help him do it.

In April 2013, Zuckerberg also launched a new lobbying group, FWD.us, which had three core aims: immigration reform; improving state education; and enabling more technological breakthroughs of benefit to the general public. FWD.us was backed by a number of Silicon Valley entrepreneurs, and its first President was Zuckerberg's friend, Joe Green. The lobbying group is not aligned to a particular political party. It favours the bipartisan approach and though there is some positive evidence of its impact on policy (TechCrunch reported that FWD.us drove 33,500 calls to Congress in summer 2013, and a total of 125,000 actions including social media shares), that is less than the founders might have liked. Other criticisms of FWD.us is that it has a poorly defined long-term agenda, and doesn't articulate its vision well.

↳ Be open about the issues that are important to you, and use your platform to advocate change.

In terms of other politically charged issues which he cares about, Zuckerberg has openly supported gay and trans-gender rights, riding with Facebook's carnival float at the annual San Francisco Lesbian, Gay, Bisexual, and Transgender Pride Celebration in 2013. In the aftermath of the Paris terror attacks in December 2015, he spoke out in support of the Muslim community, explaining that he wanted "to add my voice in support of Muslims in our community and around the world" and reminding others that "as a Jew, my parents taught me that we must stand up against attacks on all communities." Zuckerberg has also voiced his support for the Black Lives Matter campaign, explaining in a memo to staff that "*Black Lives Matter* doesn't mean other lives don't – it's simply asking that the black community also achieves the justice they deserve." The memo was a response to his discovery that some Facebook employees crossed out Black Lives Matter graffiti, overwriting it with All Lives Matter. He was angry about this fact, on the grounds that the very act of crossing something out "means silencing speech, or that one person's speech is more important than another's."

Twelve

Personal Life

Zuckerberg is still only 34 years old, and so the timeline of his personal life is correspondingly short. We discussed his early years in *Childhood and Education*, and so this can only really consider his personal relationships and religion.

Nothing much is known about Zuckerberg's teenage dating exploits, though that might well be because his forays into relationships were few and far between. He met Priscilla Chan at a frat party in his sophomore year at Harvard, where she was also studying, and the couple started dating in 2003, a year before the birth of Facebook.

↳ Find a partner who is your equal, in life as well as in business and shares your values.

Chan was born in Braintree, Massachusetts, and grew up just outside Boston. The oldest of three sisters, her parents were Chinese refugees, who arrived in the US on the Vietnamese refugee boats. As a child she spoke Cantonese at home.

Though quiet and usually in the background, Chan is as smart as Zuckerberg, which is no doubt what attracts him to her. She was her class' Valedictorian in high school, and she graduated from Harvard University with a BA in biology, and a minor in Spanish. On graduating, she taught science for a year, then went on to medical school at the University of California. She graduated in 2012, married Zuckerberg the same year, and works as a paediatrician. It is likely that it is Chan who pushed for the focus on health at the Chan Zuckerberg Initiative.

↳ Personal loss can happen to any of us, however much money we have.

Maxima Chan Zuckerberg (Chén Míngyû, to give her Chinese name) was born on 1 December 2015, and her parents presented her to the world with their announcement of the Chan Zuckerberg Initiative (see *Philanthropy*). The baby, known as Max, was long-awaited: Chan had suffered from three previous miscarriages, and so it was inevitably with trepidation that the couple announced her pregnancy, and relief when the baby arrived safely.

Zuckerberg blogged to his 33 million followers about Chan's miscarriages. Although there were those who felt this was over sharing, plenty more were positive about his honesty. He wrote:

We hope that sharing our experience will give more people the same hope we felt and will help more people feel comfortable sharing their stories...

Most people don't discuss miscarriages because you worry your problems will distance you or reflect upon you – as if you're defective or did something to cause this. So you struggle on your own.

For anyone, a man in particular, to speak out about the pain and loneliness of losing a child (and, in this tragic case, three children), took many by surprise, but has hopefully opened up a forum for others to discuss what they have been through, and to find support online. It also moves Zuckerberg from his pedestal as a godlike figure in the tech world, and reveals to both his fans and his detractors, that he too is a mortal, capable of misfortune and suffering like any other man.

Conclusion

“*Some people dream of success, while others wake up and work hard at it.*”

—Mark Zuckerberg

Not all of us can be like Mark Zuckerberg. Intellectually, he is far ahead of most of his Harvard University peers, let alone the general public, and his breadth of interests and knowledge – from art history to Latin – is unquestionably unusual too. There are only a certain number of Facebooks which can be founded in any generation, one man at a time can be *Time* magazine's Person of the Year, and with $46 billion currently behind him (and more with every passing day), Zuckerberg indisputably has an advantage on the average man on the street.

But that is not to say that his personal attributes, his values and interests, and the career path he has chosen cannot be a source of inspiration to us all. There are plenty of lessons we can learn from him, and apply in our own lives, which will put us in a stronger position intellectually, personally, financially, and in business.

If we were to summarise the content of this book into four unforgettable lessons from Mark Zuckerberg, those lessons would have to be as follows:

1. If you have an idea, develop it. And if it doesn't work out, have another idea, and develop that one too. Eventually you will come up with an idea that you are satisfied with and which is commercially viable.

2. When you have found that idea, focus on it. Zuckerberg has focused on Facebook every single day for over a decade. It's taken a great deal of blood, sweat and tears, not to mention brain power, to get this far.

3. Remember that human communication and interaction are the most powerful and emotional channels we have. If you can tap into our desire and need to engage with one another, in a way which is effective but unobtrusive, you have the basis for a successful company.

4. Give back to the society you live and work in. No one succeeds on their own, and whether you are at

the top of your game, or still climbing the ladder, you have a responsibility to contribute your time, money, energy, and ideas to making the world you live in, a better place.

Even if you live and sleep work, you still need someone in your life to support you when things are tough. Don't overlook your personal life if you want to be truly rich.

Think carefully about what you can do, in each aspect of our life, to apply Zuckerberg's lessons. Your ultimate goal is not just to make money, but to be fulfilled, and to play a positive role in the world. Zuckerberg is a role model for us all.

JAICO PUBLISHING HOUSE

Elevate Your Life. Transform Your World.

ESTABLISHED IN 1946, Jaico Publishing House is home to world-transforming authors such as Sri Sri Paramahansa Yogananda, Osho, The Dalai Lama, Sri Sri Ravi Shankar, Robin Sharma, Deepak Chopra, Jack Canfield, Eknath Easwaran, Devdutt Pattanaik, Khushwant Singh, John Maxwell, Brian Tracy and Stephen Hawking.

Our late founder Mr. Jaman Shah first established Jaico as a book distribution company. Sensing that independence was around the corner, he aptly named his company Jaico ('Jai' means victory in Hindi). In order to service the significant demand for affordable books in a developing nation, Mr. Shah initiated Jaico's own publications. Jaico was India's first publisher of paperback books in the English language.

While self-help, religion and philosophy, mind/body/spirit, and business titles form the cornerstone of our non-fiction list, we publish an exciting range of travel, current affairs, biography, and popular science books as well. Our renewed focus on popular fiction is evident in our new titles by a host of fresh young talent from India and abroad. Jaico's recently established Translations Division translates selected English content into nine regional languages.

Jaico's Higher Education Division (HED) is recognized for its student-friendly textbooks in Business Management and Engineering which are in use countrywide.

In addition to being a publisher and distributor of its own titles, Jaico is a major national distributor of books of leading international and Indian publishers. With its headquarters in Mumbai, Jaico has branches and sales offices in Ahmedabad, Bangalore, Bhopal, Bhubaneswar, Chennai, Delhi, Hyderabad, Kolkata and Lucknow.

SINCE 1946